Here are some other
nonfiction chapter books you will enjoy:

Caves!: Underground Worlds
by Jeanne Bendick

Earthworms: Underground Farmers
by Patricia Lauber

Exploring an Ocean Tide Pool
by Jeanne Bendick

Frozen Girl
by David Getz

Frozen Man
by David Getz

Great Whales: The Gentle Giants
by Patricia Lauber

In Search of the Grand Canyon:
Down the Colorado with John Wesley Powell
by Mary Ann Fraser

Life on Mars
by David Getz

Lighthouses
by Brenda Z. Guiberson

Mummy Mysteries:
Tales from North America
by Brenda Z. Guiberson

Salmon Story
by Brenda Z. Guiberson

Spotted Owl:
Bird of the Ancient Forest
by Brenda Z. Guiberson

TALES OF THE HAUNTED DEEP

TALES OF THE HAUNTED DEEP

BRENDA Z. GUIBERSON

Henry Holt and Company ⚓ New York

For Doug and Katy,
always looking for great adventures
in the big city

Thanks to all who helped get this book through its various phases, including Jeremy D'Entremont and Claudia A. Jew, and a special thanks to Margaret Garrou, Tim Travaglini, and many others at Holt.

Henry Holt and Company, LLC, *Publishers since 1866*
115 West 18th Street, New York, New York 10011

Henry Holt is a registered
trademark of Henry Holt and Company, LLC

Published in Canada by Fitzhenry & Whiteside Ltd.,
195 Allstate Parkway, Markham, Ontario L3R 4T8.

Library of Congress Cataloging-in-Publication Data
Guiberson, Brenda Z.
Tales of the haunted deep / Brenda Z. Guiberson.
p. cm.
Includes biographical references and index.
Summary: Nonfiction accounts of ships that sank inexplicably,
and other mysterious maritime occurrences.
1. Curiosities and wonders—Juvenile literature. 2. Shipwrecks—Juvenile literature.
3. Sea stories—Juvenile literature. 4. Ghost stories—Juvenile literature.
[1. Curiosities and wonders. 2. Sea stories.] I. Title.
G557.G85 2000 001.9'4—dc21 99-34976

ISBN 0-8050-6057-X / First Edition—2000
Designed by Nicole Stanco
Printed in Mexico

1 3 5 7 9 10 8 6 4 2

CONTENTS

TALES OF THE HAUNTED DEEP

CHILLS FROM THE SEA

Ghost stories are as old as language and more frequent than a new mystery. Their images shimmer like hot air over a flame as storytellers reach for words that might explain the unknown. What is that great flash of light in the sky? What makes the wind suddenly blast and bellow? What happens when someone dies? Could that be a monster rising from the depths?

The best ghost stories begin with something real. A feared pirate dies in a bloody battle, but no one seems to forget him. A mariner sees an unknown creature and can't resist telling his friends about the "great slimy thing that leave a track where he been, ugly eyes, scales all over him." Manatees have inspired mermaid stories, and long-toothed narwhals have become unicorns. Fossilized shark teeth were once thought to be the tongues of serpents turned to stone. As such stories are told and retold, they become legends of the sea.

Ghostly sea stories are filled with horror, creepiness, delight, and even humor. A strange creak on a ship, a lighthouse that flashes without being lit, a misty figure on the beach that leaves no footprints—these are as fascinating as a locked door. We want to know about them even as our hearts flutter and our blood turns icy cold.

The lives of early sailors, lighthouse keepers, and pirates were filled with ghost stories because these people living in close contact with the sea faced constant danger. They saw great ships break apart against the rocks, whole crews die of sickness and starvation, and strange creatures pop their heads out of the water or wash up on the beach. Sea monsters were often drawn on the ancient maps of the world. Stories of ghosts and monsters helped people of earlier times explain the vast power and mystery of the sea.

Ancient mariners had many ideas about keeping themselves safe during long sailing journeys. Most

Wreck of the French ship Alice *near Ocean Park, Washington, January 1909.*
Courtesy of the Columbia River Maritime Museum, Astoria, Oregon, neg. no. 1964.73.

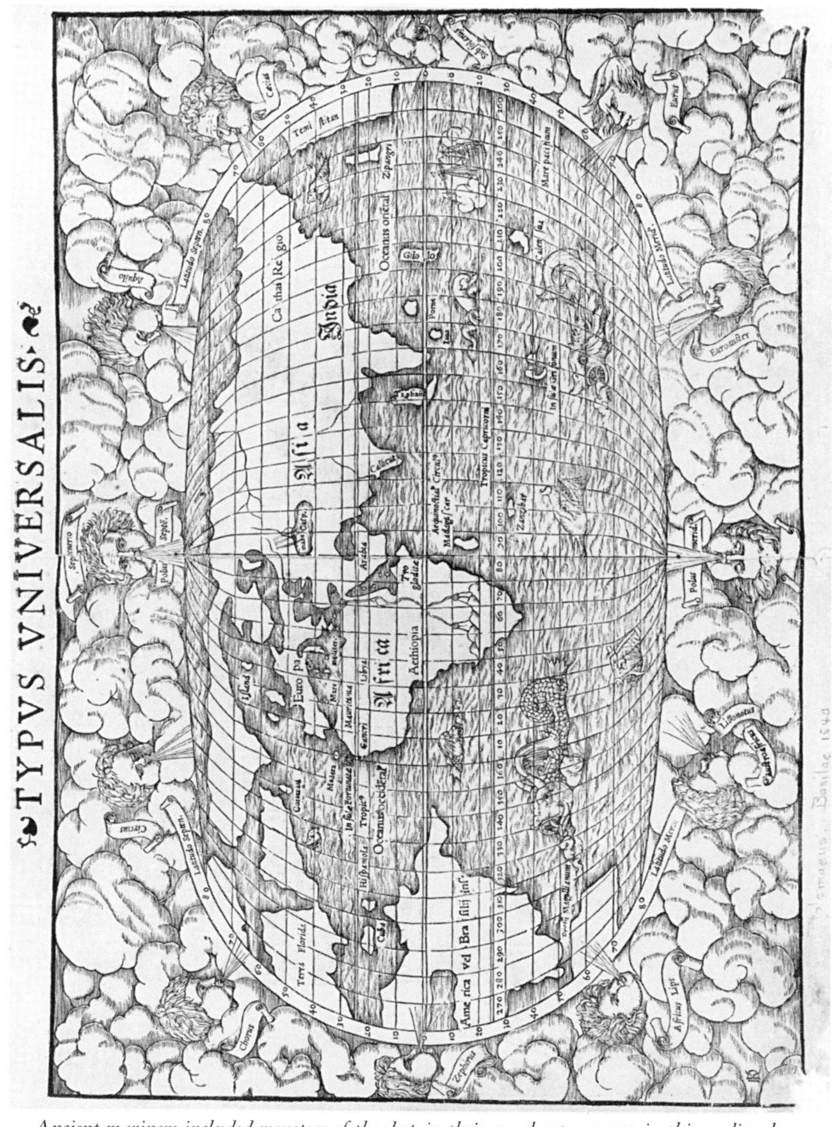

Ancient mariners included monsters of the deep in their sea charts, as seen in this medieval map of the world drawn in 1540. Courtesy of the Mariners' Museum, Newport News, Virginia.

would refuse to sail on a ship with a coffin aboard. They felt a dead body could attract violent storms, blinding fogs, and killer waves. A crew might mutiny if the body was not quickly sewn into a canvas and thrown overboard with heavy shackles to make it sink. As the ship's sail maker sewed up the canvas, the last stitch was passed through the dead person's nose to keep the shroud in place. No one wanted the corpse to rise up to haunt the living.

Mariners never started shipbuilding on a Thursday, the day named for Thor, the Norse god of storms. They believed using oak wood could keep lightning away. They built figureheads on ships so that the staring eyes, the soul of the ship, might offer some protection.

The crews on sailing ships were always at the mercy of the wind. A hurricane could sink them. No wind at all could leave them starving and dying of thirst in a dead calm. They thought a large bird called an albatross could affect the wind, so they would never kill one for food. Some captains hung "bags of wind" near their cabin door in case they needed it. Others carried strings with three knots.

Undoing the first knot might stir up a fine wind. Opening the second knot could turn it into a gale. But undoing the third knot might unleash a hurricane, something only a reckless and arrogant captain would want to do. Too much whistling on board could also bring on a hurricane. According to one old sailor, "We only whistle when the wind is asleep." Few sea wives would dare to blow on oatcakes hot out of the oven because they believed their breath might call up a great storm.

Sailors felt that the sea would eventually take them to their deaths. They hung iron horseshoes or wore gold earrings to protect themselves from drowning. Most never learned to swim because they did not want to die a slow watery death. Sailors were convinced their end was a bed on the cold ocean floor, where fish would pick at their eyeballs and coral would grow into their bones. They called this grave Davy Jones's Locker. *Davy* may come from the word *duffy,* a slave term for "ghost." *Jones* may refer to Jonah who was, according to the Bible story, sacrificed to the sea by sailors anxious to escape a storm. *Locker* is another term for a seaman's chest, where things can be stored.

Occasionally a sea ghost emerged to offer a friendly warning, but mostly, sailors feared ghosts as creatures who would lure mariners to their doom. Friendly or not, sea ghosts seem unable to rest. They appear again and again over misty waters, surging into new stories like waves breaking across the beach. Pale and dripping, with moans and groans, sea ghosts continue to haunt sailors, and their stories chill the hearts of all who will listen.

Sailors fear a permanent visit to Davy Jones's Locker at the bottom of the sea.

THE DREADED PIRATE GHOSTS

It is 1717, and an unarmed English merchant ship, heavily loaded with silk and molasses, makes its way toward a Virginia harbor. Suddenly it is approached by a speedy sloop, also sailing under the flag of England. Is it friend or foe? The merchant ship captain is alarmed when the lookout reports cannons on the deck. In another minute, the second ship shows its true colors, whipping down the English flag and hoisting a black banner displaying a skeleton and a bleeding heart. The merchant ship captain groans and mutters. His crew doesn't stand a chance. The flag belongs to Blackbeard, the fiercest pirate ever to sail the Atlantic coast.

Blackbeard was a pirate for only two years but was very bold and terrible. During that short time, he managed to accumulate four ships, forty cannons, a crew of 140 seamen, fourteen wives, and considerable treasure. Little is known about his early life except that he was born Edward Teach of Bristol, England, and learned how to handle ships during the War of the Spanish Succession, which ended in 1713.

He started his pirate life in 1716. He became known as Blackbeard, as he let his hair get shaggy and beard grow until people said it grew up to his eyelids and covered his ears. Before battle, he draped smoldering cords over his long braids to look dangerous as the smoke curled up around his face.

Blackbeard's flag.

Although Blackbeard's career as a pirate was relatively short, his fearsome visage and ruthless attacks earned him a legendary reputation. Courtesy of the Mariners' Museum, Newport News, Virginia.

Blackbeard burned ships, marooned sailors, and killed those who refused to join him. When it came time to divide treasure, he abandoned and killed his sailors until only a few men were left to share the wealth.

In the fall of 1718 Blackbeard hid in a pirate camp by the shallow water near Ocracoke, North Carolina. He then attacked and looted ships that tried to pass by. The local governor and others tolerated him because he sometimes shared his plunder with them. But many people, including Alexander Spotswood, governor of Virginia, were tired of pirates. Spotswood sent Lieutenant Robert Maynard to capture Blackbeard.

Maynard managed to trick the pirate. When Blackbeard fired cannons, Maynard ordered some of his men to hide below deck. As smoke and wood splinters clouded the air, Blackbeard did not see this maneuver and told his pirate crew to jump aboard Maynard's ship. British sailors then swarmed up from the hold for a bloody battle. Maynard and Blackbeard fought each other with pistols, swords, and fists. The pirate suffered twenty stab wounds and five shots but kept fighting. Finally he collapsed from loss of blood.

Blackbeard's head was cut off and hung from the bowsprit at the front of the ship. The headless body was thrown into the sea. The legend of his ghost begins here. It is said that the head screamed loudly at Maynard while Blackbeard's body swam one time, two times, then three times around the sloop before sinking into the deep.

Since that time, Blackbeard's ghost has remained headless and reportedly returns often to haunt the cove on Ocracoke Island, now called Teach's Hole. Local fishermen say they have seen the headless figure floating on the surface of the water. It swims round and round three times in the moonlight. It glows with a pale shimmering light called phosphorescence. At times it comes ashore with a lantern, searching endlessly for the missing head. The old pirate's boots leave no footprints. Any strange light seen on this beach today is called "Teach's Light."

What happened to Blackbeard's skull? As a warning to other pirates, it hung for many years on a pole in the James River in Virginia. Eventually it was taken down, coated with silver, and used as a large

After Blackbeard was killed, his head was hung from the bowsprit. Legend has it that the head screamed while the headless body swam three times around the ship before sinking beneath the waves. Courtesy of the Mariners' Museum, Newport News, Virginia.

drinking cup at an old college fraternity. Later it was taken to a tavern. The local silversmith reportedly engraved *Deth to Spotswoode* on the rim, remembering Governor Spotswood of Virginia who sent out the men to capture Blackbeard. Many people were challenged to drink from it over the centuries and then it seemed to disappear. A judge who saw the cup on Ocracoke Island in the 1930s later offered $1,000 to find it again but had no success.

Recently what is thought to be Blackbeard's silver-plated skull was donated to the Peabody Essex Museum in Salem, Massachusetts. It came from the collection of Edward Rowe Snow, a twentieth-century author of many books on Atlantic coast shipwrecks, lighthouses, pirates, and treasures. He was well known from lectures and radio shows, and over

People claim that Blackbeard's headless ghost still walks the beach near Ocracoke, North Carolina.

the years he received 13,000 letters about hidden treasures and unusual sea stories. Eventually the clues led him to find two buried pirate treasures. He also succeeded in tracking down the skull of Blackbeard.

Snow told a friend a good story about the skull. One night when he was alone with the skull and trying to write a new chapter, he just couldn't concentrate. The wind was loud and persistent, but he heard a soft voice say, "'Tis a dirty night to be off a lee shore—get to the pumps, you dogs." He turned

Historian Edward Rowe Snow is shown holding Blackbeard's silver-plated skull.
Reprinted by permission of Dorothy Snow Bicknell.

around expecting to see a visitor, but the room was empty. Then he heard, "Get a reef in that sail, you lubbers—do yer want your bones to bleach on the beach?" Was he working too hard? Imagining things? No one was in the room. Then Snow looked at the skull on the windowsill and asked, "Are you the person who just spoke to me?"

"I am not a person" was the reply. "Formerly I was a person—a person of importance. Possibly you have heard of me. I was Captain Teach."

The skull admitted that he had buried treasure, and Snow asked for clues. The skull said he planted a chest at Cape Hatteras, North Carolina, but also killed the two men digging the hole and pushed them in. He wanted them to "hold that pot o' gold down for me and the Devil." The skull mentioned another treasure buried on a beach near three oak trees, but a terrible lightning flash ended the conversation before Snow could get better details.

Blackbeard's hidden treasures are still a mystery. The night before he died, Blackbeard told a friend that "nobody but me and the Devil knows where my treasure is buried and the one what lives longest will

get it all." The pirate may have buried silver bars and gold coins on Smuttynose Island, Maine. He left his sixth wife behind on the remote island to watch over his affairs. Through the centuries, residents report that her ghost continues to haunt the island. Is she guarding a treasure? In the early 1800s, Captain Samuel Haley dug up five bars of silver there.

There are many ghost stories about pirates and their chests full of jewels and valuable coins, such as pieces of eight and gold doubloons. They hid them in caves, coves, and lonely sandy beaches and would do almost anything to keep others from finding the stash before they could return.

Captain William Kidd, hanged as a pirate in 1701, may have buried many treasures, including some found on Gardiners Island near New York City. Kidd marked his chests with the initials *W. K.* and had a sailor dig a hole in the sand to bury them. Then, like many other pirates, he killed the sailor and pushed him into the hole. In this way he created a ghost to forever guard his treasure.

During this time Hannah Screecham lived with her sister on a small island just off the coast of Cape Cod.

Whenever a pirate hid treasure on this island, Hannah provided a ghost to guard it. One day Captain Kidd came ashore with a sailor and a treasure chest. The captain paid Hannah with a ring, a shawl, and a strand of his own hair. Then Hannah led the sailor far across the island to bury the treasure while Kidd waited. After the sailor put the chest into the hole, Hannah shoved the man into the pit and buried him. Then she screeched like a terrified gull being tossed about in a storm. When the wind carried the sound to Kidd, he

Captain Kidd would stand watch while one of his crew dug the pit and buried his treasure. The crewman would then be murdered so he could never reveal the location of the treasure, and his ghost would stand guard over it forever.

shuddered. But he knew that his treasure was safe and he sailed away. Today if anyone looks for gold buried on Screecham's Island, Hannah still shrieks to warn Captain Kidd as he sails by in his ghostly ship.

Ghosts connected with Kidd's treasure were sometimes called "candle ghosts." In the 1700s, people tried to lure these ghosts out with a burning candle and a promise of "a place of untroubled rest." They wanted to see the ghost emerge from the ground so that they could locate the treasure. Today treasure hunters are more likely to use a metal detector or sonar.

How can a ghost protect a treasure? It's easy. According to legend, if the ghost causes anyone to speak or scream, then *poof,* the treasure vanishes.

The sea is full of dramatic events that leave people startled and gasping for breath. Some of the stories involve monstrous creatures with toothy heads, slippery tails, and a great deal of body in between. These unidentified swimming objects have poked their heads out of the water on the East Coast, the West Coast, and in deep cold lakes all across the country.

SWISH, SWIRL, SEA SERPENT

August 1817, Gloucester, Massachusetts. On a warm afternoon Timothy Hodgkins is sailing into the harbor with three friends. Ahead of them they see what seems to be a school of pilot whales. As they get closer, they are shocked. The whales now look like the humps of a sea monster. Hodgkins can count "twenty bunches" of humps. He says that the sea monster is huge, "not less than one hundred and twenty feet" with a body "the size of a sixty- or eighty-gallon cask." Others who have seen it describe a creature at least fifty feet long with "a head as large as the head of a horse." The eyes are "frightful and glaring . . . nearly as big as the rim of a middling sized tea-cup." It moves with "the motion of a caterpillar" and has "very thick scales and its appearance very terrific."

A Boston newspaper gives it a headline: A MONSTROUS SEA SERPENT: THE LARGEST EVER SEEN IN AMERICA. Those who have spotted the creature agree. Those who have not seen it are skeptical—isn't this just imagination gone wild, stories created from a swirling ripple of the sea?

Whatever it is, the creature continues to poke its head out of the water. The Gloucester fishermen worry that this hungry monster could eat all the fish, and a reward is posted. When the creature is spotted near the Squam Lighthouse, the whole

The original caption read, "Sea serpent: Engraved from a drawing taken from life as appeared in Gloucester Harbour, August 23rd, 1817." Courtesy of the Mariners' Museum, Newport News, Virginia.

whaleboat fleet goes out for the hunt. Swish! It slips away from them into the unknown watery depths.

Three days later, Captain Richard Rich, a whaleboat commander, harpoons something in the harbor. It pulls him about fifty yards. When the ship stops, the captain hauls up the harpoon, but it dangles empty over the glistening water. Where did the creature go? Is it real? For the next few weeks, many people continue to report it. One captain says he was able to look into the creature's gaping mouth and see teeth like a shark's.

As sightings of the Gloucester sea serpent continue, the Linnaean Society of New England decides to investigate. Although monstrous sea creatures have been reported around the world for hundreds, even thousands of years, this is the first time anyone has taken a scientific look at the mystery. They ask witnesses twenty-five questions, with the written answers sworn to before a justice of the peace.

After two serpents are seen together, the committee wonders if perhaps the creatures have come close to shore to lay their eggs. In September two boys

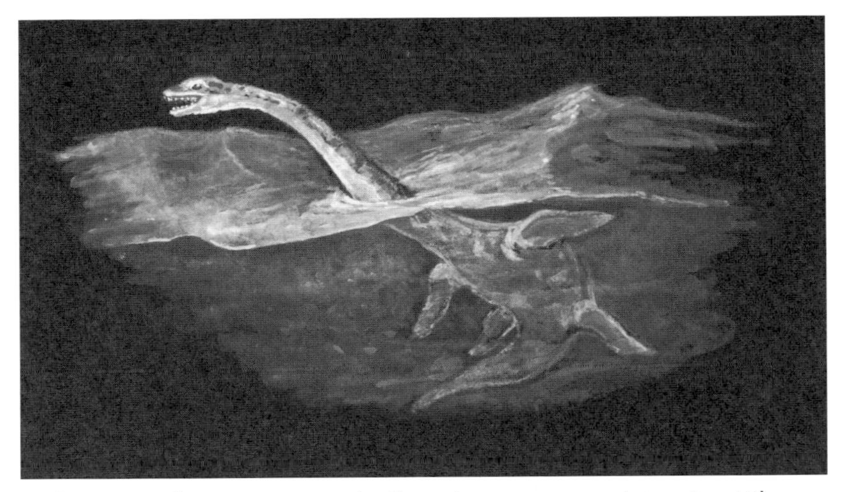

Some reports of sea creatures seem to describe an elasmosaurus, an ancient marine reptile that is thought to be long extinct.

playing on a beach at nearby Cape Ann find a three-foot snake with humps on its back. The investigating committee decides that this must be the sea serpent's baby! The "baby monster" gets a big name, *Scoliophis atlanticus,* which means "Atlantic humped snake." For a short period they have proof for the skeptics who do not believe. Soon, however, a naturalist who specializes in reptiles examines the specimen and makes a correction. This snake is a *Coluber constrictor,* a blacksnake, a bit deformed but *very* common. Because of this one mistake, the scientific investigation is no longer considered dependable.

Skeptics begin to call the serpent "Embargo," which is a backward spelling of *O Grab Me*—something most imagine will never happen. Many conclude that the serpent is simply a disturbance in the water caused by a large fish.

But the sea serpent continues to appear in the area. Similar sightings are made in Maine, South Carolina, and many places along the Atlantic coast for years, even up to the present time. Some descriptions are exaggerated, others are obvious hoaxes, but there are also many witnesses who make clear, consistent reports that seem very reliable. None of the reports can offer final proof that the monster truly exists. It remains fascinating and elusive, just beyond anyone's ability to classify or touch it. It is a wonderful mystery of the sea.

Was the Gloucester sea serpent one of those "unknown animals," which occasionally puzzle the scientists when they make an appearance? Was it a sea ghost with ripples but no substance? Was it the only one of its kind?

Sea monsters have been sighted all over the world for centuries and were even drawn on ancient maps.

Across the United States, thirty-eight states claim water monsters lurking within their borders, and there are plenty more in Canada. Many of these creatures have long existed in Indian legends. The Kwakiutl Indians told of a sea monster named Yagin, who devoured men, brought on storms, and destroyed whole tribes. The Manhousat people of Vancouver Island, Canada, spoke of Hiyitl'iik, a sea serpent about eight feet long, quick on either water or land, and able to grow wings. Along the coast of

A ceremonial mask used by the Kwakiutl, a native North American tribe, depicts the face of Yagin, a sharklike monster of the sea, who devours men, brings on storms, and destroys whole tribes.
Photo by Eduardo Calderon, courtesy of the Burke Museum of Natural History and Culture, Seattle, Washington, catalog no. 1-1451.

the Pacific Northwest, its image was put on native boats and tools and carved into rock as drawings, which are called petroglyphs. Other sea monsters continue to be reported in this area today.

Like the well-known Loch Ness monster of Scotland, many unidentified creatures pop up in deep, cold lakes. One that has been reported numerous times lives in Okanagan Lake in British Columbia. In a legend from the Okanakane tribe it is called N'ha-a-itk, the "Lake Monster." The story is connected with the killing of "Old Kan-He-Kan," an old man whom everyone loved. The gods punished the murderer by changing him into Okanagan Lake so that he could do no more harm. As the story goes, his spirit lived on in the water, stirring up great

Ancient petroglyphs, or rock carvings, of sea monsters found on Vancouver Island, British Columbia.

storms and even gulping down two horses that tried to cross the lake. When tribal members paddled across the lake, they always carried a small animal to drop into the water to keep the spirit happy. It is said the spirit is ashamed to show his face.

In 1926 H. F. Beattie wrote a new verse for an English song because he wanted to have a little fun with the lake monster. After the song was performed at a luncheon on the shores of Okanagan Lake, the monster had a new name and international fame.

I'm looking for the Ogopogo,
The bunny-hugging Ogopogo.
His mother was a mutton, his father was a whale,
I'm gonna put a little bit of salt upon his tail.
I'm looking for the Ogopogo.

Two months later people claimed to have seen Ogopogo again. The ferry service in the area made serious plans to equip their new boat with "devices designed to repel the attacks of Mr. Ogopogo and family."

Ogopogo never attacked anything and gradually

came to be described in more friendly terms. Many do not believe that Ogopogo exists, however, unless they are one of those who have seen it. A tugboat captain named Jack McLeod traveled the lake for twenty-seven years without noticing anything unusual. Then, in 1949, he saw a fast-moving creature with a great wake behind it. "At last I've seen Ogopogo," he said. "This is no second-hand story, as I saw it with my own eyes." In 1968 a water-skier named Sheri Campbell almost hit Ogopogo floating without its head or tail being visible. "I became a little hysterical," she said. "I had no idea where his mouth was!" With her teenage friends, they chased the monster at forty miles per hour in the boat but were unable to keep up.

Walter Wachlin and his children, Randy and Sheri, saw Ogopogo while they were on vacation in 1981. They describe the huge creature as snakelike, with "scales and fins on the top that had laid down." It had "several humps like a camel" and "moved up and down very fast, like a caterpillar." It created a large wake that "was swirling around as if it were boiling." In that amazing encounter, thirteen-year-

Could this photograph taken by thirteen-year-old Sheri Wachlin be the elusive Ogopogo of Okanagan Lake? Reprinted by permission of the Walter Wachlin family.

old Sheri was able to take four pictures with her Instamatic camera.

Ogopogo has companions named Manipogo, Sicopogo, and Igopogo living in nearby lakes. Manipogo has reportedly been seen in a rare family group of three and is said to holler, hoot, weep, and whistle across the lake. There is also another creature in the Pogo family called Saskipogo. No one has actually seen this monster. People in the Saskatchewan area felt left out of the fun and mysterious lore of sea monsters, so they made one up. Saskipogo is described as a bizarre mix between a goldfish and a wombat.

One scientist studied hundreds of sightings of sea monsters and concluded that there must be several different types of creatures among them. Do we have any idea what they might be? In 1938 an ancient fish called a coelacanth, thought to be extinct for 70 million years, was caught in the Indian Ocean. What a surprise for science! This discovery was like finding a dinosaur walking around in the backyard. If this fish could survive so long undetected, could there be other creatures that have also escaped our notice? One possibility might be an elasmosaurus, a sea reptile also thought extinct for 70 million years. Another possibility might be a relative of the zeuglodon, a whale species thought to have become extinct 30 million years ago. Could they still exist?

Some sea monsters might belong to a family of creatures as yet undiscovered. The megamouth shark was not known to science until 1976, when an adult male got tangled up in the anchor chain of a U.S.

The ancient coelacanth was believed to be extinct for 70 million years until someone surprisingly caught one in 1938. More of these fish have been discovered in recent years.
Photo by Lloyd Ullberg, Special Collections, California Academy of Sciences.

Navy ship near Hawaii. The fifteen-foot fish had never been observed before because it usually swims very deep, with its mouth wide open to filter plankton. No females or young have yet been seen.

In 1977 eighty divers made a thorough search of Okanagan Lake, looking for Ogopogo, but they found no proof. As science comes up with deeper diving machines and better detection devices, some of the mysteries of the sea may be solved. But not everyone wants this. A mysterious monster can explain the unexplainable, stir our imaginations, and frighten and thrill us all in a moment. As one newspaper man put it, "What would the Okanagan be without the Ogopogo?" The vast waters that cover the earth may be the last hiding place where a huge monster could live in peace.

People familiar with the sea are the ones most likely to experience its unusual events. Lighthouse keepers lived right at the ocean's edge. They saw and heard many things that were hard to explain. For centuries the misty air swirling around lighthouses has been carrying a large share of the ghost stories of the sea.

THE LIGHTHOUSE GHOSTS

Lighthouses were built near jagged rocks and shallow sandbars to warn ships away from dangerous places. Keepers made sure the light in the lantern burned all night and during every dark and violent storm. Still, the sea and the wind are powerful forces, and lighthouse keepers saw many shipwrecks, risked their lives in rescues, and sometimes had to retrieve dead bodies from the water. Surrounded by tragedies, lighthouses are filled with ghosts. While one ghost delivers a warning, another wanders endlessly on the beach. Still others show up just to slam a door, creak on a staircase, and perhaps move a teapot if they don't like where it is set.

Almost any small stretch of coastline seems rich with lighthouse ghosts. In 1894 in Oregon, for instance, a story surrounds Yaquina Bay Lighthouse. According to one version, Muriel Trevenard, a girl without a mother, is sailing with her father and his crew along the Oregon coast. Because the sea is rough, her father stops at Yaquina Bay and asks an innkeeper to care for her until he can return. Muriel stays at the hotel, but as the weeks drag into months, she becomes lonely and often watches for the return of her father. Sometimes she creates pictures of the sea and carefully draws his sloop sailing back into the harbor.

The haunted Yaquina Bay Lighthouse on the Oregon coast.
Photo by Brenda Z. Guiberson.

Eventually she meets some new friends, including a boy named Harold Welch. She, Harold, and their friends decide it would be fun to explore the abandoned lighthouse on the hill. The innkeeper reluctantly provides a key but warns them not to stay after dark. The lighthouse is said to be occupied by a ghost named Evan McClure. He was a violent, red-haired sea captain who was banished from his ship and set adrift by a mutinous crew. Evan and his small boat eventually perished on the rocks near Yaquina Bay. Not long after that, the boarded-up lighthouse became the source of nightly noises, strange flashing lights, and weak calls for help.

For Muriel and the others, this ghost story makes the lighthouse seem even more intriguing. They can hardly wait to open the lock. Inside, the windows rattle and hollow echoes make them shiver. They push away wispy spiderwebs to look into the kitchen and other rooms on the first floor. They climb up the steep staircase to the lantern room. At the top Muriel can see miles out over the ocean, but her father is nowhere in sight. As the group heads back down, they notice a small door barely three feet tall in the back of a room. Harold pries it open and discovers a huge black hole. He strikes a match and the light falls down, down, down into the shaft. It never seems to hit the bottom. Terrified, the group runs down the stairs, tripping over one another as they scramble to get outside.

Muriel catches her breath and suddenly realizes that she has left her handkerchief in the lighthouse. Because it was a gift from her father, she feels she must go back for it. Her friends beg her not to go, but she insists and says she will catch up with them

Muriel and her friends found a small door in the lighthouse. Behind the door was a seemingly bottomless black hole.

in a few minutes. As the others start slowly down the hill, the sky darkens, and a thick blanket of fog creeps in. Suddenly they hear screams of terror and quickly return to the lighthouse. The door is locked but Harold soon gets it open. "Muriel!" he calls. "Muriel!" But she does not answer.

Harold discovers drops of blood on the staircase. The group follows him up to the second floor, where they find a bloody handkerchief near the small door. The door is now closed tightly, and they cannot pry it open. After looking in all the rooms, they run back to town and get everyone to come with lanterns. The search continues all night and into the next day, but no trace of Muriel is ever found. Her father never returns to the harbor and is never seen again.

Today Yaquina Bay Lighthouse is a museum, brightly painted and furnished with rope beds, kerosene lamps, and a hand-operated water pump. No one is allowed up to the third-floor lantern room, but now and then a visitor points to a shadowy figure seen at the window. Or someone will report feeling a strange push when no one else is around. And many, including the Coast Guard, have seen an occasional flash of light from a lighthouse that has not been in operation since 1874.

Over the years, the stories of Muriel persist and expand. Recently an unemployed hitchhiker camping near the lighthouse was awakened by a soft light. A woman in a long dress came down the steps to him and said, "Don't worry, Harold. You are welcome here." "I'm not Harold," he said, but she didn't seem to hear. Before she went back to the lighthouse, she told him he would find a good job in Newport the next morning. And he did.

Farther down the Oregon coast, a ghost named Rue lives at Heceta Head Lighthouse. She may be the mother of a baby girl who died there. Near the lighthouse is a large house built for two lighthouse keepers and their families. The house has two of everything, including two attics. The north attic belongs to the ghost of Rue. It can be reached only by climbing up a steep ladder and squeezing through a small locked trapdoor at the top of a closet.

When Rue travels through the house, she leaves a scent of lavender behind. This may be why she didn't care for the smelly box of rat poison left in her attic in the 1950s. The box quickly disappeared and was replaced by a silk stocking from the 1890s. In the 1970s, a workman was up in the attic trying to make repairs. Every time he put his tools down, they seemed to disappear or move to another place. Frustrated, he wondered how he would ever complete the job. Then he saw the ghostly image of a woman in old-fashioned clothes floating past him. It was too much. He refused to return to the attic but was finally persuaded to work on the outside of the

The Heceta Head Lighthouse and keeper's house on the Oregon coast.
Photo by Brenda Z. Guiberson.

house. Then he accidentally broke an attic window. Glass clattered to the attic floor. He fixed the window but would not go back inside to clean up the broken fragments. That night, the residents heard *sweep, sweep, sweep* coming from the attic. When they checked in the morning, the glass shards were in a neat pile but no broom was in sight. Was it Rue, cleaning up the drafty place, trying to keep the attic as she liked it?

In the 1990s, Mike and Carol Korgan moved in to take care of the house. Mike kept losing a seaman's hat given to him by his daughter. Whenever he took it off, the hat somehow got moved to other places and was very hard to find. One day he thought the hat was lost for good. He looked everywhere and called all over town. Later, on a rare trip up into Rue's attic, he saw it on the floor. Feeling that maybe she didn't care much for this hat, he stopped wearing it.

One morning he was eating oatmeal for breakfast but got up to get something from the kitchen. His wife then left to answer the phone. When they returned, milk had been poured into his oatmeal bowl, something he never did. A few weeks later, when he went to the doctor, tests showed that he should be adding calcium, a mineral found in milk, to his diet. Was Rue now giving out advice about his eating habits?

Another time a workman was hired to add insulation to the drafty house. The job was progressing well until the workman got to Rue's attic. He managed to get one section covered, and then he quit, racing down the steep ladder so fast that he left all his tools behind, including an expensive staple gun. He never returned, and he refused to talk about what happened. Today the attic is only partially insulated, with several rolls of thick insulation waiting for anyone brave enough to install them. Perhaps Rue's attic is as it should be, drafty so that the wind can howl, cold so that an icy breath can chill those sitting in the parlor below. Hopefully the house is big enough because when the new caretakers moved in a couch and mirror from their former home in Portland, they apparently brought along a new ghost they know as John, a former owner of the Portland house. Long ago their young daughter saw him and described him as a man in a white robe, with fiery eyes, and gold feet. She saw him as he led her safely from a fire.

It is not unusual for a ghost to be involved in good deeds. For instance, visitors to Point Lookout Light in Maryland sometimes experience unusual lights or sounds. One sleeping visitor was awakened by a ring of small whirling lights on the ceiling. She watched them for a moment and then smelled smoke. Quickly she was able to put out a fire before the flames had a chance to spread.

Keepers who lived in the second Minot's Ledge Lighthouse near Boston (the first one fell over in a storm) had a similar story. Long ago they used to "talk" to each other from different rooms by tapping on the pipes. One evening they were all together eating dinner. A clammy wind whistled around their legs and fluttered across the table. They hardly noticed it. Then the wind kicked up and great waves began to crash and rumble against the tower. Still they kept eating. Then they heard a persistent loud tapping above them in the lantern room. It was so loud, they could not ignore it.

Grumbling, they left their dinner and went up to investigate. No one was at the top, but the keepers had walked into a very dangerous situation. The lantern door was wide open and swinging wildly on its hinges. At any moment a great blast of wind could have damaged the lantern and snuffed out the light meant to guide the mariners safely around the rocks. Quickly they closed up the door and were very grateful for the tapping.

On the outside of this same lighthouse, a wet, ghostly figure has been reported hanging from the ladder when a storm is brewing. He waves and

The Minot's Ledge Lighthouse near Boston—people claim that when a storm is brewing, a ghost clings to the ladder and shouts, "Keep away! Keep away!"

shouts his warning: "Keep away, keep away!" He may be a keeper who died when the first Minot's Ledge Lighthouse fell into the sea. "Keep away," he moans. "Keep away."

Perhaps he's warning us of phantom ships haunting the deep. Floating, drifting across the waves, ghostly ships are another part of the legends of the sea.

GHOSTLY SHIPS WITH A MIND OF THEIR OWN

Through the ages, mariners have passed down a warning in the event that you see the ghostly ship called the *Flying Dutchman:* Warning! Do *not* speak to the captain. If he asks your position, shrug your shoulders. If he begs for water, point to the sea. And most important, if he pleads with you to deliver letters to his wife, do not take them or your ship will never reach the safety of a harbor.

Mariners of many nations have seen and feared this *Flying Dutchman.* Its captain, Vanderdecker, is someone who looks for hurricanes to speed his ship along and bring misfortune to others. This arrogant man will do anything to get what he wants. In the seventeenth century, he spent nine weeks trying to sail around the Cape of Good Hope in terrifying weather. His crew begged him to stop. Instead the captain screamed at the wind, and, as the story goes, made a pact with a glowing figure that appeared on the deck. In their next run against the wind, the entire ship and crew were destroyed and doomed to sail the seas forever as punishment for the captain's reckless pride.

In 1881 a sailor who later became King George V of England saw the ghostly ship and recorded it in his log. "The *Flying Dutchman* crossed our bow. A strange red light, as of a phantom ship all aglow . . . masts, spars and sails of a brig two hundred yards distant. . . . When we arrived, there was no sign of any material ship. Thirteen persons altogether saw her." On this day, the man high in the mast who first spotted the ghost ship fell to his death on the deck below.

Another such legend began on a cold day in January 1646. A three-masted vessel called *Fellowship* sailed out of the harbor at New Haven, Connecticut, cheered on by all the people who lived in the town. After several years of failures and disappointments, they had loaded this ship with everything they could collect—wheat, peas, beaver skins, and silver dishes from their homes, hoping to sell it all in England. They were trying to build a new shipping trade and a better life.

The *Fellowship* was very small, and Captain Lamberton called it "cranky" because it did not turn well in the sea. Still the townspeople fitted it with new masts and sails and watched proudly as the ship sailed off with all their hopes for the future. Many prominent people went along for the journey, and those left behind waited patiently for their ship to return. They waited the entire year and well into the next year. By spring, they were rushing to ask questions of every new ship crew who came into the harbor: Have you seen the *Fellowship*? Did it ever arrive in England? Maybe you saw it drifting in distress across the Atlantic? The answer was always the same. No one had seen it. The townspeople began to pray for those most likely lost at sea and hoped that they might find out what happened.

On a bright hot day in June 1647, the townspeople witnessed a strange event, which was recorded by three historians of the time. First, there was a violent thunderstorm, which drenched them until only a few heavy clouds were left to slowly change shape over the water. An hour before sunset, a few citizens came back outside and noticed an odd cloud floating toward New Haven. As the cloud drifted lower and lower, it appeared to be in the form of a ship. The people followed it and gradually realized that it was a particular vessel. It was the three-masted *Fellowship.*

As the news passed through town, the streets filled with people watching the *Fellowship* sail above as if it were on a billowing wave of the sea. The ship came so close that one man said he could toss a stone onto the deck. Everything was so clear that the townspeople could identify the new masts and sails and even tall Captain Lamberton standing in the bow.

In the next moment, everyone gasped. The strong ship was suddenly shattered by an invisible storm. The masts snapped, the deck cracked, and the ship tilted on its side. Then, in a tangle of dangling ropes and shredded canvas, the *Fellowship* sank into the cloud until it totally disappeared.

Everyone was quiet. They had wanted to know what had happened to their ship, and now they could

The ill-fated Fellowship *is said to have appeared in the clouds over New Haven, Connecticut, in June 1647.*

only nod their heads in sad understanding. Most took up farming for the next few years before they could revive much interest in the shipping trade.

Another ghost ship comes from the Grand Banks off Newfoundland. The water there is cold and deep and a great place for cod fishing. The strong winds and currents, however, make it a dangerous and risky business. Between 1830 and 1892, nearly six hundred ships and more than three thousand lives were lost in this area alone.

During this time a ship called the *Charles Haskell* was built just for cod fishing, but the ship got off to a terrible start. Before it could be launched, a workman slipped and broke his neck. As cod fishers regarded the death as a sign of bad luck, the captain and the crew quit immediately. The ship sat in the harbor for an entire year before Captain Curtis of Gloucester, Massachusetts, finally agreed to take her out.

In the deep water of the Grand Banks, the *Charles Haskell* dropped anchor near a hundred other boats all competing for the same fish. But as the wind whipped up huge waves, the *Haskell* had to cut loose from her anchor. The captain tried to control the ship, but the fierce winds rammed it into the *Andrew Johnson.* With terrified cries, the twenty-six fishermen of the *Andrew Johnson* sank to a watery grave. The *Haskell* managed to stay afloat and sail back to Gloucester. The local fishermen now regarded this ship with more suspicion than ever. It had caused great destruction, and the captain's hands were stained with the blood of lost men. And how had the captain and crew managed to survive the terrible collision? Once again, it was almost impossible to get anyone to sail the *Charles Haskell.*

Captain Curtis was still willing, and the next spring he took the ship back to the Grand Banks.

For six days the fishing was very good. Then, in the darkness of the midwatch, a sudden chill crept in over the *Haskell.* Pale, dripping figures began to emerge from the murky depths. One by one, twenty-six silent and ghostly seamen climbed onto the ship to join in the catch. With cold, blank eyes, they sat on the benches and dropped shadowy bait and line into the sea to fish for cod. At sunrise they began to shimmer and fade. One by one, they flowed like dripping water over the side of the ship and sank back into the sea.

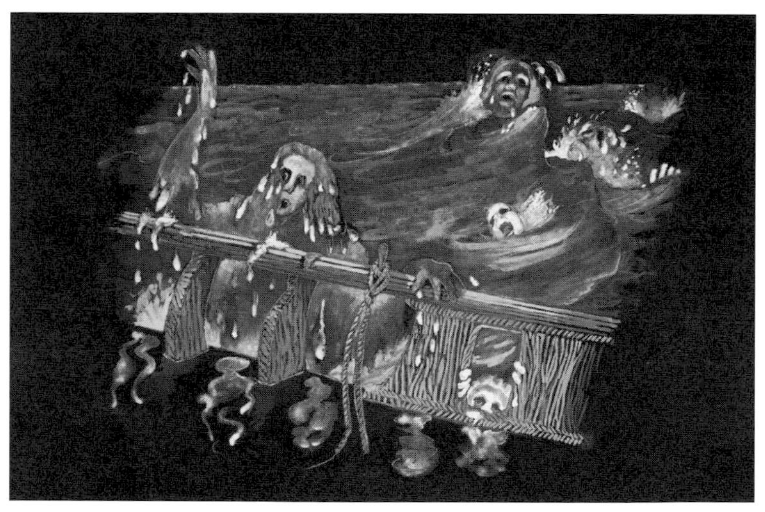

In the middle of the night a ghostly crew of drowned seamen climbed aboard the cursed ship Charles Haskell *and fished until dawn.*

Captain Curtis immediately headed back to Gloucester. The next night, just before they could reach the harbor, the ghostly crew reappeared. They passed through the ship, with cold glassy stares for the trembling captain, and then climbed over the rail. Without a ripple or a splash, they crossed the water to Salem.

From that time on, no crew would even consider taking out the *Haskell,* and the ship slowly rotted at the Gloucester pier.

Great ships are not the only ghost vessels of the sea. A very different type of tale involves an old man who lived in an icy village of the Arctic. He did not like the sounds of singing. If there was a drum dance, he left in a run. If a woman was singing, he told her to be quiet.

One day, however, he heard singing that he liked. He liked it so much that he could not help listening. The beautiful sounds came from the crew of a boat moving against the wind. But the crew was not rowing. They were singing. The man watched closely and several times he thought the boat seemed to dance in the air. He paddled his kayak toward it until he could hear the words more clearly. "Let us fly through the air, *ah, ha, aja . . .*" "Lovely," he said and the crew asked if he wanted to join them. When the man said yes, they tied his kayak to their boat.

The man began to rise with them into the sky. He sang loudly with the others as they flew over mountains until they landed on a very high peak. Here the men lived with their wives, who were eagles. They made him feel at home and then loaded his kayak with seal meat, fat, and rabbits. Then they told him he must continue his journey alone.

The man climbed into his kayak and started to sing. Soon he was flying through the air all by himself. He flew around for days and enjoyed watching the whole world beneath him. He felt very clever,

As the man sang, his kayak flew through the air.

the only one in his village who could do such a thing. He decided to fly home and show off this great ability. But as he turned his kayak, he forgot the words to the song. *"Imakaja, ha, ha . . ."* No, that wasn't it. He tried other words, but none of them worked. His kayak was falling to Earth. He tossed out the seal meat, fat, and rabbits, but he continued to fall. At the last moment he remembered the words and was able to fly the kayak again. He did not stop until he crashed through the door of his own little hut. After that he never flew again, and no one ever heard him singing.

The stories of the sea are rich and varied. They burst up from the shipwrecks and spread in the billowing storms. They blink with every flashing light as they wait to be told and retold. Will a new sea monster emerge? Is that a ship with a mind of its own? What is that rap, rap, rapping on the lighthouse steps? The stories will not end as long as someone will continue to tell them.

YOU TELL THE STORY

1

You are walking out to the lighthouse, and a sharp wind comes up. It pushes you against the railing. Then you see the lantern flash before you have had a chance to light it. Is there a ghost in this lighthouse? You tell the story.

Photo by Jeremy D'Entremont.

2

You are a visitor to this boat, exploring the galley below. Suddenly you hear the engine start up. You rush to the engine room, but it is empty. The gauge says the engine is *off.* Still you hear the motor, and the boat is moving away from the pier. What's the story?

Photo by Brenda Z. Guiberson.

Photo by Brenda Z. Guiberson.

3

You are amazed to find this old picture taken on a Seattle beach in 1906. You once saw a similar unidentified creature in the area but were afraid no one would believe you. Now you feel like telling the story. Does your sea serpent need a song?

CORBIS photo.

4

Design a flag for your pirate. How about a treasure chest? Is there a ghost to protect the gold doubloons? Does the pirate still roam the ocean as a ghost? What's the story?

These are some of the symbols used on pirate flags.

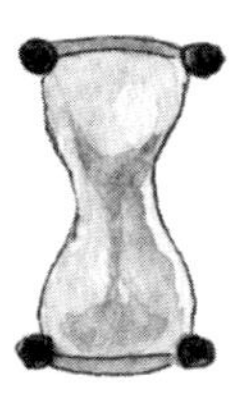

Hour glass:
"Time is running out."

Skull and crossbones:
"Death."

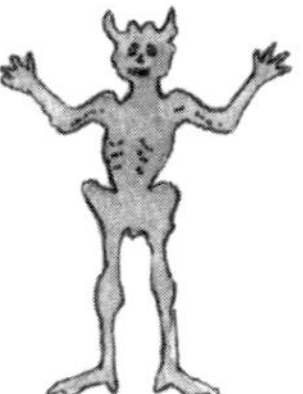

Skeleton:
"Torment."

Arrow:
"Violent death awaits."

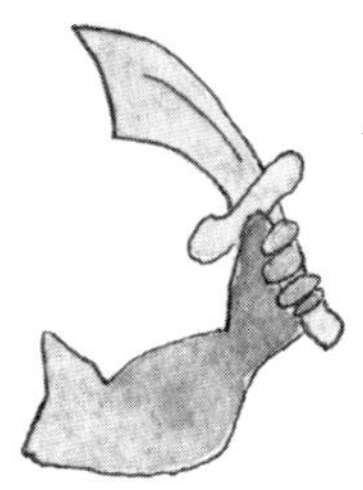

Raised arm:
"Ready to kill."

Bleeding heart:
"Slow, painful death."

5

A ship skims across the top of a wave. You are startled by this ship. Two years ago you saw it break apart in a storm and sink into the sea. Who was on this ship? Does it have a mind of its own? What's the story?

Courtesy of the Columbia River Maritime Museum, Astoria, Oregon, neg. no. 1986.54.10.

BIBLIOGRAPHY

American Folklore and Legend. Pleasantville, New York: Reader's Digest Association, 1978.

Bolté, Mary. *Haunted New England.* Riverside, Connecticut: Chatham Press, 1972.

Cohen, Daniel. *The Encyclopedia of Monsters.* New York: Dodd, Mead, 1982.

Coleman, Loren. *Mysterious America.* Winchester, Massachusetts: Faber & Faber, 1983.

Cordingly, David. *Under the Black Flag: The Romance and the Reality of Life Among the Pirates.* New York: Random House, 1995.

De Wire, Elinor. *Guardians of the Lights: Stories of U.S. Lighthouse Keepers.* Sarasota, Florida: Pineapple Press, 1995.

Dolan, Edward F., Jr. *Great Mysteries of the Sea.* New York: Dodd, Mead, 1984.

Ellis, Richard. *Monsters of the Sea.* New York: Alfred A. Knopf, 1994.

Gaal, Arlene. *Ogopogo: The True Story of the Okanagan Lake Million Dollar Monster.* Surrey, B.C.; Blaine, Washington: Hancock House, 1986.

Garinger, Alan. *Water Monsters: Great Mysteries, Opposing Viewpoints.* San Diego: Greenhaven Press, 1991.

Gordon, David G. "What Is That?" *Oceans* (August 1987): 44–49.

Helm, Mike. *Oregon's Ghosts and Monsters.* Eugene, Oregon: Rainy Day Press, 1994.

Helm, Thomas. *Monsters of the Deep.* New York: Dodd, Mead, 1962.

Heuvelmans, Bernard. *In the Wake of the Sea-Serpents.* New York: Hill & Wang, 1968.

LeBlond, Paul H., and John Sibert. *Observations of Large Unidentified Marine Animals in British Columbia and Adjacent Waters.* Vancouver: Institute of Oceanography, University of British Columbia, 1973.

Lee, Robert E. *Blackbeard the Pirate: A Reappraisal of His Life and Times.* Winston-Salem, North Carolina: John F. Blair, 1974.

Lehn, W. H. "Atmospheric Refraction and Lake Monsters." *Science* (13 July 1979): 183–85.

Lincoln, Margarette. *The Pirates' Handbook.* New York: Cobblehill, 1995.

Mackal, Roy P. *Searching for Hidden Animals: An Inquiry into Zoological Mysteries.* Garden City, New York: Doubleday, 1980.

Millman, Lawrence. *A Kayak Full of Ghosts.* Santa Barbara: Capra Press, 1987.

Moon, Mary. *Ogopogo.* Vancouver: J. J. Douglas, 1977.

Mysteries of the Unexplained. Pleasantville, New York: Reader's Digest Association, 1982.

Mysterious Creatures. Alexandria, Virginia: Time-Life Books, 1988.

Nesmith, Robert I. *Dig for Pirate Treasure.* New York: Devon-Adair Company, 1958.

Ocko, Stephanie. "The Gloucester Sea Serpent." *American History Illustrated* (April 1982): 36–41.

Platt, Richard. *Pirate.* New York: Alfred A. Knopf, 1994.

Pyle, Howard. *Howard Pyle's Book of Pirates.* Mattituck, New York: Amereon House, 1903.

Snow, Edward Rowe. *Pirates and Buccaneers of the Atlantic Coast.* Boston: Yankee Publishing, 1944.

———. *Strange Tales from Nova Scotia to Cape Hatteras.* New York: Cornwall Press, 1949.

———. *True Tales of Buried Treasure.* New York: Dodd, Mead, 1960.

———. *True Tales of Pirates and Their Gold.* New York: Dodd, Mead, 1962.

Taylor, Leighton. *Sharks of Hawaii: Their Biology and Cultural Significance.* Honolulu: University of Hawaii Press, 1993.

Wall, Dorothy, and Bert Webber. *Yaquina Lighthouses on the Oregon Coast.* Medford, Oregon: Webb Research Group, 1994.

Water Spirits. Alexandria, Virginia: Time-Life Books, 1985.

Whedbee, Charles Harry. *Blackbeard's Cup & Stories of the Outer Banks.* Winston-Salem, North Carolina: John F. Blair, 1989.

INDEX

(Page numbers in *italic* refer to illustrations.)